A PUFFIN BOOK

PROPERTY OF

ELLA rose
Bigmore

JOYCE LANKESTER BRISLEY (1896–1978) wrote and drew books from an early age; she had her first fairy story published in a children's paper at the age of thirteen. She studied at art school and, when she was twenty, had pictures hung in the Royal Academy. She is the author and illustrator of the well-loved Milly-Molly-Mandy stories, adored by little girls everywhere.

JOYCE LANKESTER BRISLEY

A PUFFIN BOOK

PUFFIN BOOKS

UK | USA | Canada | Ireland | Australia
India | New Zealand | South Africa
Puffin Books is part of the Penguin Random House group of companies whose
addresses can be found at global.penguinrandomhouse.com.

www.penguin.co.uk
www.puffin.co.uk
www.ladybird.co.uk

First published by George G. Harrap & Co. Ltd 1937
Published in Jane Nissen Books 2005
Reissued in this edition 2016

001

Set in 12.5/16.5 pt Sabon LT Std
Typeset by Jouve (UK), Milton Keynes
Printed in Great Britain by Clays Ltd, St Ives plc

A CIP catalogue record for this book is available from the British Library

ISBN: 978-0-141-36867-2

All correspondence to:
Puffin Books
Penguin Randon House Children's
80 Strand, London WC2R 0RL

Penguin Random House is committed to a
sustainable future for our business, our readers
and our planet. This book is made from Forest
Stewardship Council® certified paper.

Contents

BUNCHY
and the
PASTRY-DOUGH

ONCE upon a time there was a little girl called Bunchy, who lived with her grandmother in a cottage in the country.

It was a pretty little cottage, with roses climbing over it; and it had a pretty little garden with sweet peas and sunflowers growing in it; and there was beautiful country with woods and meadows lying all around it.

So Bunchy was a happy little girl, living there with her kind old grandmother.

There was only one thing missing, which was that she had nobody to play with.

The cottage was a long way from the village, and hardly anyone came so far along the road except the miller with his sacks of flour, or the peddler with his tray of needles and buttons, or the grocer with his packets of tea and sugar.

But never anyone who could stop and play with a little girl like Bunchy.

One day Grandmother had to go to market, leaving Bunchy to keep house alone, for it was rather rainy for her to go along too.

Grandmother put on her cloak and her bonnet, her galoshes and her mittens, took her big basket and her big umbrella, and set forth. And Bunchy stood in the little rose-covered porch, waving goodbye, feeling rather lonely, for she didn't know how she could manage to pass the hours by herself till Grandmother returned.

Grandmother got as far as the gate, and then she suddenly remembered something. And she stopped and called back to her granddaughter:

'There's a small lump of uncooked pastry-dough on the larder shelf, which was left over when I made the pie this morning. If you would like to have it to play with while I am gone, you may, my dear.' (For she knew how Bunchy always enjoyed standing by the kitchen table making things with little bits of dough while her grandmother was rolling the pastry.)

'Thank you, Granny,' called Bunchy, still waving from the doorway; and Grandmother waved her umbrella for the last time before she went out of sight behind the hedge, on her way to market.

Then Bunchy turned back into the house.

She wandered upstairs, and she wandered downstairs, and she looked out of all the windows (not that there were many stairs or windows in the little cottage). And then, not finding anything interesting to do anywhere there, she thought that perhaps she would get out Grandmother's piece of dough and play with it.

So she went to the larder. And there on a plate on the shelf was a little round lump of pastry-dough, soft and cold, waiting to be moulded into anything a little girl could fancy.

Bunchy took it into the kitchen, rolling it between her hands, and she put it on the table, and pressed it out flat and rolled it up again several times.

'What fun it would be,' said Bunchy to herself, 'to make a little pastry-girl to play with!'

So she got a knife from the basket, and, standing on a stool, started cutting out a little girl from the flattened dough on the table, beginning at the top of the head, all down one side, arm, and leg; then up the other leg and the other arm, up till she reached the head again.

And when the knife reached the place where it had made the first cut, and the little pastry-girl was quite complete – what *do* you think happened? Why, the little pastry-girl lifted her head from the table and sat up; and while Bunchy, still standing on the stool, watched, with her mouth wide open in surprise, the little pastry-girl pulled her legs from off the table and jumped down with a soft thump on to the kitchen floor!

'Well!' said Bunchy to herself, staring with all her might. 'Well, well, well!' (Which was what her grandmother always said when surprised, but there didn't seem to be anything else to say!)

The little pastry-girl began stretching herself as if she were doing exercises, but Bunchy soon saw that she was trying to get her arms and legs more to the same length, for Bunchy had really made them rather odd. Then the pastry-girl began feeling her pastry-head with her pastry-hands, and Bunchy suddenly thought:

'Why, I haven't given her any face!' So she quickly got the currant-box from the cupboard, took out two currants, and pressed them into the little pastry-girl's head, for eyes. Then she took a tiny knob of dough from the table and pressed it into the centre of the pastry-girl's face for a nose. And then with a spoon she made a line below it for a mouth.

And in a trice the little pastry-girl was smiling and twinkling at her in the friendliest way possible!

Here was a quaint playfellow!

Bunchy was delighted, and amused herself for some time by making pastry buttons down the front of her dress, to finish her off; and as each one was set in place the little pastry-girl looked so pleased.

Presently Bunchy gathered all the odd scraps of dough together into a ball. And, strangely enough, they made a lump which seemed as big as the first one. She rolled it out flat again.

This time she thought she would make a pussy-cat; so she cut out a fine big one, head and ears and paws and tail all complete. And when it was done, up it got and down it jumped on to the floor, waving its white pastry-tail from side to side.

This *was* fun!

Bunchy stood rolling together the left-over bits of dough while she watched her pastry-girl and pastry-cat making friends.

Strangely enough, the dough ball seemed still to be quite as big as before, so Bunchy rolled it out yet again on the table.

This time she thought she would make a house. So she cut out a house, with a roof and chimneys, and a door and windows, all complete, while the little pastry-girl and the cat looked on, very interestedly. And when the last window was cut out and the house was finished it reared itself upright on the table and slipped down on to the floor; and it grew and grew, until at last it was quite of a size to admit people like Bunchy herself.

As she stood there staring up at it, the little pastry-girl slipped one chilly hand into hers and drew her towards the front door. The pastry-cat ran in before them, leading the way into a little white kitchen, with a table and chairs and a dresser and crockery all made of pastry-dough (which surprised Bunchy, for she had not made any 'inside' to the house).

The pastry-girl pulled out a chair for her, and Bunchy sat down carefully. She felt as if she were sitting on a piece of cold, soft india-rubber.

There was a shining black kitchen-range at one end of the room, with a warm glow of fire in it, just like the one in Grandmother's kitchen; in fact, somehow Bunchy thought it *was* that same one, though how it got into the pastry-house, or whether the kitchen itself had turned into pastry, or if the pastry-house were still standing in the kitchen, she couldn't make out.

While she was puzzling over it the little pastry-girl picked up the pastry-cat and set it on top of the stove. Bunchy was afraid it would be too hot there, but it settled down quite contentedly, while the little pastry-girl fetched plates from the dresser and set them on the table.

Bunchy sat watching them both, and presently she noticed that the pastry-cat was slowly turning to

7

a golden-brown colour. The next minute the pastry-girl had taken it from the stove, broken it in crisp pieces, and piled them on the plates on the table.

Then she signed to Bunchy to draw up her chair and eat, and in some surprise Bunchy did so.

The pastry-cat tasted very good, and Bunchy crunched away until she had eaten up all the pieces; for the pastry-girl only pretended to eat (having, of course, no proper mouth), and when she had pretended enough over one piece would slip it on to Bunchy's plate and take another.

When the meal was finished the pastry-girl led the way up some funny soft rubbery stairs to the little bedroom above.

Here was a white pastry bed, with a thick pastry-coverlet; and the little pastry-girl at once pulled her buttons off (which were the only things she could remove) and got into bed, making room for Bunchy to get in beside her.

But Bunchy didn't want to get in – the bedclothes looked so cold and sticky. Still the little pastry-girl kept beckoning and patting the lump of pastry which served for a pillow.

Just at that moment there was a distant bang of a door shutting. Was it Grandmother, come home from market?

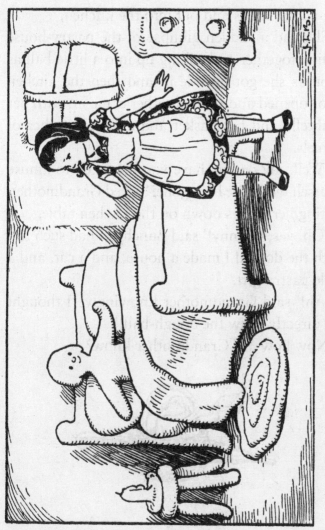

Bunchy didn't want to get in

Bunchy turned and ran from the room, down the pastry-stairs and out into the kitchen.

She had a sudden glimpse of the pastry-house falling together and rolling up into a little ball as soon as she got outside it; and then the kitchen door opened and Grandmother came in, with her umbrella and her basket and a great number of parcels.

'Well, my dearie, have you managed to amuse yourself while I've been gone?' asked Grandmother, setting her things down on the kitchen table.

'Oh, yes, Granny!' said Bunchy. 'I had such fun with the dough! I made a house, and a cat, and a little pastry-girl.'

'Ah!' said Grandmother knowingly. 'I thought so, directly I saw the dough-ball!'

Now how *did* Grandmother know?

BUNCHY and the CUTTING-OUT SCISSORS

ONCE upon a time the little girl called Bunchy was again left all alone in the house, while her grandmother went to see an old friend who lived in the village some distance away.

Grandmother was sorry to have to leave Bunchy alone, but she had not been to see her old friend for a long time, and she knew it would cheer her to have a nice basket of flowers and some fresh eggs brought to her.

So Grandmother packed a basket, while Bunchy fetched Grandmother's bonnet and cloak and black cotton gloves, all ready to put on. And then when Grandmother was ready Bunchy went with her to the front door, wondering rather, to herself, what she could do to make the time pass till her grandmother came back again.

Well, Grandmother got as far as the gate, and then she suddenly remembered something, and she turned and called to her little granddaughter:

'Bunchy, on the shelf by my armchair there is a sale catalogue, and in the pocket of my work-basket you will find an old pair of scissors. If you would like to cut out while I am gone, you may, my dear.'

'Thank you, Granny!' said Bunchy. And she stood waving from the doorstep until her grandmother was out of sight behind the hedge on her way to the village.

Then Bunchy turned back into the house.

She went into the kitchen, and there on the shelf by Grandmother's big armchair was a paper book full of pictures of pretty ladies, and gentlemen, and furniture, and all sorts of things. So Bunchy quickly got the scissors out of the pocket of Grandmother's big workbasket, and settled herself down in Grandmother's big armchair for a nice game of cutting-out.

She began on a lady in a dainty pink dressing-gown trimmed with white fur, because she thought her the prettiest of all.

Carefully she snip-snip-snipped with Grandmother's scissors in and out all the way round the pink lady, until the scissors arrived again at the place where they had started.

And then – what do you think? – why, the little lady jumped down on to the floor, fluttering her pink wrapper, and, seating herself gracefully on the footstool, began tidying off the little odd scraps of white paper which Bunchy had carelessly left on her edges.

'Well, well, well!' said Bunchy delightedly, staring at the pink lady. 'Now I must cut out some more, so that she will have plenty of people to play with!'

So she set to work to cut out all the prettiest ladies, and all the gentlemen who were properly dressed or had nice dressing-gowns on. And directly each little paper-doll was cut out down it jumped and went over to the others, and they shook hands.

Strangely enough, they all looked just about Bunchy's own height when they stood down on the floor; but they were all flat one way, or the little kitchen would have seemed quite uncomfortably full of people, standing or strolling around.

Bunchy hurriedly turned the pages of her catalogue till she found some chairs and sofas, which she cut out, and then she watched the gentlemen handing the ladies to the seats. They were all so fine and elegant that they made the little kitchen look quite shabby, so Bunchy found some pictures of brightly coloured curtain materials, which she cut out. The paper-people looked very pleased and gathered them up at once, shaking out the folds, and soon had the kitchen draped around quite festively.

'Now, I wonder what they would like to do,' said Bunchy to herself. 'If they had some music they could have a ball. I wonder –'

She quickly turned the pages. Yes! There at the very end was a piano advertisement!

You should have seen the excitement of the paper-people as she cut out the piano and stood it down for them! One gentleman sat down to it at once, and began playing the most dance-y music you can imagine, and all the others ran here and there, clearing the floor for the ball. There was really not very much space for dancing, so all the gentlemen got together, and they pushed the walls of the kitchen back and back, one after another, until they had made a great spacious ballroom of it, all draped with the beautiful curtain materials.

Then while the pianist played on the paper-piano the little paper-people danced – so lightly and gracefully that Bunchy thought she would never get tired of watching them.

While she was sitting there, with the scissors and catalogue on her lap, a handsome little gentleman in a purple silk dressing-gown came up and took her hand. Bunchy saw that he was asking her to dance, and for a moment she rather wondered what to do, for she had never been to a ball before – and, besides, she was just a little afraid lest she should crumple her partner!

However, he smiled encouragingly, and all the other paper-people smiled welcomingly at her as they danced; so she rose and put her hand on the gentleman's shoulder (he was just her own height), and off they went.

The music was so thrilling, it seemed to get into her and make her feel as light as paper herself; her partner was very kind, and steered her in and out

He was asking her to dance

among the maze of dancers so cleverly that after a minute or two Bunchy felt as if she had been dancing all her life, and would never want to stop!

But presently the music ceased, and the gentlemen took their partners to the seats, and Bunchy's gentleman led her back to Grandmother's chair.

And then everybody sat around and seemed to be waiting. Bunchy wondered what for.

Then suddenly she thought, 'Perhaps they are expecting refreshments! Whatever shall I do?'

She caught up the catalogue. Ah! Here were tea-sets and coffee-sets – what a relief!

Up came the scissors, and *snip-snip-snip*, the things were cut out; and the paper-people, crowding eagerly round, were soon pouring tea and coffee from the paper-pots, and sipping daintily from the paper-cups. Bunchy also found pictured some biscuit tins and chocolate boxes, and when these were cut out and passed round it was pretty to see the

paper-people open the lids and help themselves to paper-biscuits and chocolates.

They looked so good, Bunchy wished they could have been real when her dancing partner offered her the tin at the same time that the pink lady handed her a little cup of coffee. She could get nothing at all out of the box, which was rather hard on her when all her companions were happily nibbling at the good things.

Just at that moment there came a distant sound, like an explosion, that shook the gorgeous curtains on the walls. They shrank and crumpled down in folds. The spacious ballroom closed in until it became just the little old cottage kitchen again, and all the paper-people rushed together and dwindled into a little crowd on the hearthrug.

It was the sound of the front door shutting.

In another moment Grandmother came into the room in her bonnet and cloak, with the empty basket on her arm.

'Well, my dearie,' said Grandmother, 'and has it seemed a very long time, all alone?'

'Oh, no, Granny! I've been to a ball!' said Bunchy.

'You have?' said Grandmother. 'Well, now, I expect you must be just ready for a little refreshment after it. See what I have brought home for you!'

And Grandmother brought out of her basket a nice big chocolate-cream, wrapped in silver paper.

BUNCHY and the SCRIBBLE FAMILY

ONCE upon a time the little girl whose name was Bunchy was playing on the floor, while Grandmother sat knitting in her big armchair.

Bunchy had a pencil and some odd pieces of paper, and she was busy writing.

Bunchy called it writing, though *you* might have called it scribbling; but then Bunchy had not begun to go to school yet, for the school-house was nearly a mile walk away over the hill, and Grandmother thought she was too small to go so far by herself, just yet awhile. But Bunchy loved pretending to write; and when she jumped up at intervals to show the paper to Grandmother, the old lady always seemed to understand what was meant, and (with only a very little help from

Bunchy herself) would read it out quite easily, to Bunchy's great satisfaction.

Presently Bunchy grew tired of 'writing', and started to draw.

She drew a house, which seemed the easiest thing to do – two walls, and a roof, and a front door, and a window downstairs, and another window upstairs, and a chimney with smoke coming out at the top. Then she added a path and a gate leading to it, and showed it to her grandmother.

'That's a nice cottage,' said Grandmother approvingly.

'Yes,' said Bunchy. 'But I don't know how to make people to live in it. How do you draw people, Granny?'

So Grandmother put down her knitting-needles, and took Bunchy's pencil. And on the back of an envelope she drew a nice stout gentleman with a pot-hat on and a lot of buttons down his coat. (Grandmother liked drawing the buttons best.)

'Now a lady, Granny,' said Bunchy, very interested.

So Grandmother drew a lady with a little hat on and a lot more buttons all the way down her coat.

'Now draw some children! Please, Granny!' said Bunchy.

'Good afternoon, Miss Bunchy!' he said

But Grandmother put down the pencil and took up her needles, saying, 'No, no. I can't do any more scribbles. You must do them yourself now.'

So Bunchy took the two drawings back to the hearthrug and held them side by side.

'How do you do, Mr and Mrs Scribbles!' she said. 'I'm very pleased to see you. Are you just going for a walk?'

Mr Scribbles lifted his pot-hat, and bowed politely. 'Good afternoon, Miss Bunchy,' he said. (He had to speak in rather an odd sort of voice because his mouth had been drawn crooked.) 'My wife and I were about to go for a walk to look for a nice house. Have you seen one anywhere about?'

'Yes,' said Bunchy. 'I know where there is a very nice house indeed. If you will come with me I will show it to you. It's just down this lane here.'

'Why, how very fortunate that we met you!' said Mrs Scribbles. (Her mouth was so very small that she could only talk in a kind of little squeak.) 'We have been looking everywhere for a nice place to live, but we can't find anything nice enough.'

'I think you'll like this one,' said Bunchy. 'It's a beautiful house, and it's not far off.'

So they walked down the lane (that was really the border of the hearthrug) – Mr Scribbles first, waddling along from side to side, because of his legs being fastened on at the corners; and Mrs Scribbles pit-patting along behind him on her silly little heels; and Bunchy following close, wondering how Mrs Scribbles' hat stayed on, for it was uncomfortably balanced at the very top of her head, and her arms were so short that she couldn't possibly hold it on herself. Every time the wind blew, Bunchy got ready to make herself useful and catch the hat; but, though it wobbled dangerously, somehow it just managed not to fall off.

Soon they came to the cottage which Bunchy had drawn first.

Mr Scribbles stood still in the lane. 'Why, this looks just the thing,' he said.

And Mrs Scribbles stood still beside him. 'Why, so it does!' she said.

'It's all for you, Mr and Mrs Scribbles,' said Bunchy. 'Won't you go in, please? I'm sure you'll like it.'

So Mr Scribbles held open the gate for his wife, and then they went up the little path. But he didn't open the front door, and Bunchy suddenly saw it was because there was no door-handle, so he couldn't. So she quickly drew a handle, and a knocker too. And then Mr Scribbles knocked on

24

the knocker with a loud *bang-bang*, and opened the door, and they all went in.

'What a very nice cottage!' said Mrs Scribbles, holding up her short little arms with pleasure and surprise; and they went upstairs and downstairs, looking in all the rooms and admiring everything. 'Yes, we will certainly take this house.'

And when they said, 'We must have a bed here,' or 'a chest of drawers there,' or 'a table there,' Bunchy drew it for them, till the house was all furnished to their liking.

'Now we must have a nice tea to make us all feel at home,' said Mrs Scribbles, sitting down on a chair (which was several sizes too small for her, I'm afraid), while Bunchy hastened to draw a teapot and cups and a plate of currant buns. (Bunchy wasn't quite sure whether she was supposed to be a removal man, or a housemaid, or what, but anyhow she was a very useful sort of person for the Scribbles family to have about, so it didn't matter.)

Mr Scribbles stood by the fireplace reading an envelope covered with 'writing' as if it were a newspaper, and sometimes he read bits aloud to his wife – but it seemed quite different from what Grandmother had read out before.

When the tea was ready Mrs Scribbles began to get very restless. She kept going to the window and looking out; and then she went to the front door and opened it, looking up and down the lane.

'I wonder when they'll come,' she said several times.

'Don't worry, my dear,' said Mr Scribbles, behind his newspaper. 'They're sure to be along soon.'

'Perhaps they can't find the house, and they've got lost,' said Mrs Scribbles. 'Oh, dear, dear, where can they be?'

'I expect they've been kept in after school because they've been naughty,' said Mr Scribbles sternly.

Bunchy suddenly thought to herself, 'Oh, they're looking for their children, and they aren't drawn yet!' So she got pencil and paper again,

and managed to draw a little girl. (You knew it was a little girl because she had a short skirt.) She wasn't a very pretty child, but Mrs Scribbles seemed to think her all that was lovely when Bunchy brought her along.

'Oh, my darling little girl, where have you been?' she cried, kissing her fondly.

'We lost the way,' squeaked the scribble-girl, 'and I was going to ask the way at this cottage, and then you were here, and oh! We've been walking a long, long time.'

'And where is your little brother?' asked Mr Scribbles.

'Oh, he's just coming. He won't be long. He's running as fast as he can.'

So Bunchy had to hurry and draw a little boy then; but, being in too great a hurry, she drew so badly that the Scribbles family wouldn't have anything to do with the sort of person she presently brought in to them – and really I don't blame them, for besides being extremely ugly he was a great deal bigger than Mr Scribbles himself.

'Go away! You aren't our little boy!' they cried.

So Bunchy had to try again, and this time she did better. And oh! Weren't they all pleased to see each other! The scribble-boy had to be kissed and petted too; and then both the children ran all over the cottage to look at their new home, fairly squeaking with excitement all the time.

Presently the whole family sat round the table, and Mrs Scribbles poured out tea from the rather odd-shaped teapot, which Bunchy had already drawn. She drew them a whole cottage loaf and a big pot of jam, as well as the plate of currant buns.

And do you know, the Scribbles family ate up every single little bit!

'Well, that does look a nice tea you've drawn there!' said Grandmother, stooping to look over Bunchy's shoulder. 'That teapot makes me feel quite thirsty. It must be time for our tea, I think.'

'Those are buns, Granny, look!' said Bunchy.

'Well, well! I see they are,' said Grandmother, nodding. 'Now suppose you were to get out the little rock-cakes I made this morning from the larder, while I lay the table!'

So Bunchy left the Scribbles family to put themselves to bed, while she helped Grandmother to get the tea.

'I'm glad we have real cakes and not scribble-cakes, aren't you, Granny?' said Bunchy, putting the plateful on the table.

'Oh, scribble-cakes are very well indeed in their way,' said Grandmother, 'but I think just now is the time for something a little bit more substantial, don't you?'

O NCE upon a time, one afternoon, the little girl whose name was Bunchy had to amuse herself very quietly, for her grandmother was having a nap in her big armchair by the fire.

Grandmother had had a very busy morning, ironing piles of frocks, and petticoats, and pinafores, and pillow-cases and things; so, when dinner was over and the dishes were all washed up and put away (with Bunchy's help), Grandmother thought it would be rather nice to have a little rest!

So she made up the fire, put her red shawl comfortably round her shoulders, and was going to sit down; but then she thought of something.

And she went to a cupboard and brought out her button-bag, which she gave to her little granddaughter.

'There, my dearie,' she said. 'You can play with these for a while, if you like – only don't make too much noise.'

'Oh, thank you, Granny!' said Bunchy, who had just been wondering what she could do to amuse herself; and she put the footstool under Grandmother's feet and saw that she had everything she wanted.

Then Grandmother settled down for her nap, and Bunchy settled down on the floor by the cupboard, with the button-bag.

Now the cupboard, besides being the place where Grandmother kept her button-bag and piece-bags and work-bag, had one shelf which was Bunchy's own shelf.

Bunchy hadn't many toys, so Grandmother had helped her to make the shelf look like a doll's-house. There were little chairs made of cork and pins with red wool wound round them, and a little chest of drawers made of matchboxes, and a little cardboard bed and table. And on the wall at the back were pasted little pictures, and a window cut from a coloured curtain-advertisement. So that it looked quite like a doll's-house.

Bunchy's one and only little doll, Buttercup, lived there, when Bunchy was too busy to play with her.

It must be rather lonely for Buttercup, Bunchy thought, not having a granny-doll nor any brother- or sister-dolls, when the cupboard door was shut. And very dark and stuffy too. But then there was the advertisement-window stuck on the wall, which always looked as if the sun were shining through, and Bunchy hoped Buttercup could look out of that and get some air.

Anyhow the doll was very pleased to come out now and see what Bunchy had to show her.

'Look here, Buttercup!' the little girl whispered. 'It's a sack of treasure!' And she opened the button-bag and poured the buttons out into her lap.

There were big buttons and little buttons, pearl buttons and boot-buttons, buttons of crystal and of brass – all sorts and colours. Bunchy loved Grandmother's button-bag! There were buttons strung together which had come off different dresses in the past, when Grandmother was quite young; one lot of glass which Bunchy called 'diamonds', had been on Grandmother's wedding dress. And there were some round gold ones with coloured bits in them which had even been on a dress belonging to Grandmother's mother!

Bunchy admired these most of all; she thought they looked like costly jewels, and Buttercup thought so too. Bunchy put them round Buttercup's neck and waist, and Buttercup looked like a queen!

The little doll fancied herself tremendously, and Bunchy had to wait on her like a humble slave, attending her to her throne on the cupboard shelf, where she sat before the cardboard table as if waiting for a feast to be brought.

Bunchy quickly sorted out some large flat pearl buttons for dishes, and she put on one a funny button, that looked as if made of pink custard, and set it before Buttercup, who ate it up with great appetite.

Bunchy found another button like a green jelly, and one that might have been a little brown cake. And a small red one put on top of a bigger white

33

bone one looked like a delicious raspberry tart. Buttercup was so pleased with this last that she picked out a button just like a silver medal and presented it to Bunchy.

Bunchy bowed gratefully, and pinned the medal on to her frock, knowing that she must now be a very important person.

Now whether it was that the button-medal had some magic in it, or whether Bunchy was really such an important person in doll-land, I don't know; but when Buttercup beckoned her to come in and look out of the stuck-on paper window with her, Bunchy went in at once. The doll threw open the window, and the little patterned curtains waved about in the breeze.

Bunchy looked out.

There seemed to be a tiny street outside, for there were little wooden trees and shops. The sun shone brightly down from a sky that looked as if painted on paper, but white clouds were all the while moving slowly across the blue.

As Bunchy stared between the curtains she saw a little doll go walking stiffly past down the street with a little basket on its arm, and enter the little wooden cake-shop opposite. Then a small wooden greengrocer's cart and horse drove by, laden with toy cabbages, and numbers of toy people came out of the houses and hurried round to buy cabbages from the busy little wooden greengrocer.

It was really a very interesting window, and Bunchy was so glad to think Buttercup had such a nice window to look out of. Now she need not be at all sorry for her when the cupboard door was shut.

Just then Buttercup pushed her aside and waved her china arms from the window to catch the notice of the toy people outside. They came running across with great curiosity, dropping their cabbages in all directions; and the little wooden greengrocer hurried over too.

Buttercup turned and signed to Bunchy in queenly fashion to bring over the button-plates of food left on the table.

Bunchy brought her the brown button-cake, and Buttercup loftily handed it down through the window to the people outside. What excitement there was among them! They fairly fell on the button, which soon disappeared from view, and then they handed back the empty button-plate and all looked up at the window for more.

Bunchy hastily searched among Grandmother's buttons for other suitable ones.

There seemed to be a tiny street outside

She handed out big and little cakes of all colours, and jellies, and tarts – made by putting flat red or green buttons in the middle of bone ones for raspberry or gooseberry tarts; and a large yellow button in the middle of a great white one made a fine treacle tart which was too big to go on any of the plates.

And the excitement of the toy people as they gobbled them up and handed back the plates was quite worth seeing!

When there was no more food, Bunchy handed Buttercup brass buttons for money, which the doll tossed with queenly air from the window, and watched the toy folk scrambling wildly about for it. And when there was no more of that she threw button jewels, which the toys gathered up and took home, and were rich for life!

Really, there weren't very many of Grandmother's buttons left, only a few uninteresting grey and brown and black ones.

Then Buttercup began to take off her own decorations, the 'diamonds' which had been on Grandmother's wedding-dress, and the costly 'jewels' belonging to Great-grandmother, and made as if she were going to throw them out.

But Bunchy tried to stop her.

'Oh, *no*!' she said. 'I don't know whatever Granny would say if *those* buttons went. We have to be *very* careful of those. They are tre-men-dously valuable, Buttercup!'

But Buttercup still looked as if she meant to toss them to the toy folk, some of whom were still waiting hopefully outside.

Bunchy sprang to the printed window before the doll could get to it, and quickly slammed it shut.

'Well, well!' said Grandmother, slowly getting up out of her big armchair and putting her cap straight. 'You have been a nice quiet little girl, Bunchy, my dear! And what have you been doing?'

Bunchy held up Buttercup, still hung with buttons.

'Why, she's a queen!' said Grandmother.

'Yes, Granny,' said Bunchy. 'And I guarded her jewels. And I wouldn't let her throw your diamonds out of the window, Granny. I wouldn't!'

'That's a good girl!' said Grandmother. 'Now put away all the buttons into the bag and shut the cupboard, and we'll have tea!'

BUNCHY
and her SHOP

ONCE upon a time the little girl whose name was Bunchy was playing in the garden of her grandmother's cottage all by herself, as usual.

She had a long board, resting between a wooden box and the kitchen stool, and on it she was setting out different things like flower petals, a bit of bread-crust, twigs, and other odd things found about the garden.

She was so busy arranging everything to her liking that she scarcely noticed her grandmother come out to cut a cabbage for dinner until she heard her say:

'And what is all this, my dear – a shop?'

'Yes, Granny,' said Bunchy. 'I am just going to open it. Look, Granny, I can sell everything you want: dress stuffs – this is beautiful red silk' (and she held up a poppy petal) – 'and loaves of bread' (she pointed to the crust), 'and walking-sticks –'

'A sort of general shop, then, is it?' said Grandmother. 'That's a very useful sort. I hope plenty of customers will come along soon!'

Then Grandmother went indoors again with her cabbage, and Bunchy went on fussing about her counter.

'There, now!' said Bunchy at last, in satisfied tones. 'I should think everything's about ready now. I'd better open the shop!' So she got behind the counter, and waited for customers to come.

She looked about, and presently caught the eye of a tall poppy standing close by.

'Good morning, ma'am!' said Bunchy politely. 'Can I sell you anything this morning?'

'Yes,' said the poppy; 'I should like a small piece of red silk to match my dress, please. I've torn one of my petals a little bit.'

'I believe I have just the colour to match!' said Bunchy, fetching a petal from the counter. 'Yes, it's exactly the same red! Shall I send it for you, ma'am?'

'No, thank you, I'll take it with me,' said the poppy. So Bunchy laid the petal on one of the poppy's leaves, and turned to her next customer. It was a blue lupin rather bent in the back.

'What can I sell you, ma'am?' asked Bunchy.

'I want a walking-stick,' said the lupin. 'Have you got one that will fit me? I'm feeling so bent this morning!'

'Oh, yes!' said Bunchy promptly. 'I've got a very nice walking-stick here – I'll show you. There! – Is that about the size, do you think?'

'Just right!' said the lupin. 'Now can you tie me up to it, please?'

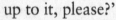

'Yes, ma'am. I'll just get you a nice piece of string, if you won't mind waiting a moment.'

'Oh, no,' said the lupin.

So Bunchy ran in and got a piece of string from the string-bag behind the scullery door. And then she carefully tied the blue lupin to the stick so that it stood up straight and looked much better.

'That's a very nice stick,' said the lupin, 'and fits me perfectly. I shall tell everyone about your shop. Good morning.'

'Thank you, ma'am, good morning,' said Bunchy, and looked round for another customer.

The next was a tired-looking pink snapdragon.

'Oh, dear! It's such a hot morning!' said the snapdragon. 'I wish I could buy a drink of water somewhere.'

'Oh, you can, ma'am!' said Bunchy. 'I have a shop just here. I'll get you some!' And she fetched the watering-can, which had a little water in it, and gave the snapdragon a good drink.

'There!' said Bunchy. 'Now you'll feel better. Perhaps you'd like a bit of shade – I'll just put this flower-pot here, so that you can sit in the shadow and cool off a bit.'

'Thank you,' said the snapdragon. 'How very useful to find a shop so near! It's a nice sort of shop – I expect you have a great lot of customers!'

'Yes, ma'am, I'm very busy indeed,' said Bunchy. 'Is there anything else you would like?'

'No, thank you, nothing more today,' said the snapdragon.

So Bunchy went back to her shop. Presently she noticed the grass border by the flower-bed; it was looking very long and untidy. She went over, and stooped down to hear what it wanted.

'Good morning,' said the grass. 'I was told you had opened a shop here. I am just wondering if

'Anything for you today, Mr Sparrow?'

you happen to do hair-cutting, because I badly
need it – my hair's getting dreadfully long; it
hasn't been done for some time.'

'Oh, yes, sir! I do hair-cutting and shaving and
everything. I can sell you a hair-cut with pleasure.
I'll just get my hair-cutting scissors!' So Bunchy
ran and fetched the gardening shears; and she
knelt down and snip-snip-snipped along the edge
of the grass, and tidied it up quite a lot; though
she couldn't do as much as she would have liked
because the shears were so hard and stiff for her
hands. Still, she made it look much better, and the
grass seemed very satisfied.

'Ah, now I feel more respectable! It does make
you feel so untidy when
your hair's too long,
doesn't it?'

'Yes, indeed,' said
Bunchy. 'Granny cuts
mine sometimes, when
it needs it. Now, is
there anything else I
can sell you? – You don't want a stick, or a drink
of water, do you?'

'Not today, thank you,' said the grass. And
Bunchy returned to her shop.

A little cock-sparrow flew down on to the ground, out of the big oak tree.

'Anything for you today, Mr Sparrow?' called Bunchy.

'No, thanks!' twittered the little cock-sparrow, rather hurriedly. 'At least,' he added, as he flew nervously on to the fence a little farther off, 'I could do with some crumbs, if you have any.'

'Of course I have!' said Bunchy. 'This is a general shop, and it sells everything. Here you are, Mr Sparrow!' She broke up the small crust from her counter into tiny pieces and threw them out on to the grass; and after eyeing them this way and that for some time, Cock-Sparrow at last flew down and caught up a bit and flew quickly off with it.

'Thank you!' he chirped, as he passed her with his beak full. 'I'll come back for another bit in a minute.' And in another minute back he came. 'This is a very handy shop,' he said, picking up a second crumb. 'My children are always so hungry it's hard to keep them fed. I didn't know where to find any more food for them.'

'I hope they'll like their dinner,' said Bunchy; and just then she heard Grandmother calling, 'Bunchy, come along in! Dinner's ready!' So she quickly shut up her shop and ran indoors.

'Granny, I've been so busy! I had lots of customers!' she said, as they began to eat.

'Did you, my dear!' said Grandmother. 'Well, I hope you've made your fortune!'

Bunchy paused suddenly.

'Why, I forgot all about money!' she said. 'But anyhow, Granny, I've been so useful – and I enjoyed it like anything!'

'Ah!' said Grandmother wisely. 'Then you haven't done badly for yourself, after all!'

BUNCHY and the SCRAP-WORK-SCREEN

ONCE upon a time the little girl named Bunchy was sitting with her grandmother in the little cottage kitchen.

It was raining hard, so Bunchy could not go out to play. She had been indoors doing lessons with her grandmother all the morning, spelling and writing; and now that she couldn't go out, and had no one to play with, she didn't quite know what to do with herself.

'I wish I had a picture book, Granny,' she said.

'Yes, dearie, I wish you had,' said Grandmother thoughtfully, over her knitting-needles. 'Don't you want to look at my old screen any more?'

'I've looked at it, and looked at it, till I've looked it all up now, Granny,' said Bunchy.

'But if I opened it so that you could see the inside, that would be newer, wouldn't it?' said Grandmother, putting down her knitting and going over to the corner of the room by the dresser, where the old screen stood.

Now, the old screen had been decorated with scrap-work pictures by Grandmother and her two sisters, years and years ago, when they were girls together at home.

Bunchy knew so well, for she had heard the story often, how the three had collected pretty coloured pictures for a long time, all their friends and relations helping. And then how Grandmother and her two sisters (Bunchy's great-aunts) had set to work cutting out the pictures so carefully, round every rose petal or child's curl, and pasting them cleverly one against another all over the screen, so that each fold looked like one big, glorious picture. And then, when every bit was stuck and dry, how Grandmother's father (Bunchy's great-grandfather) had painted a coat of beautiful shiny varnish over it all; and the scrap-work screen was finished!

Grandmother had been very proud of the screen in those days. But now it looked shabby and faded; the pictures at the edges were getting torn, and the shiny varnish was turning brown.

There wasn't much room for screens in the little cottage, so it had to stand folded up by the kitchen dresser, and the only side that showed had got gradually darker and dirtier, with dust and knocks, and the touch of Bunchy's fingers, as she traced the outlines of the pictures she knew by heart and made up stories about them.

But the inside folds, which were nearly always closed up – they were clean and almost as bright-coloured as when new.

So now, when Grandmother opened out the screen right across the dresser, and pushed the table aside so that Bunchy should have more light, the little girl eagerly knelt on the ground before it, looking for dimly remembered favourites.

Yes; there were the three lovely Spanish ladies, with their big black eyes and their yellow dresses and lace mantillas; and there was the girl skating, in a long red coat and an enormous hat and muff; and there was the tall man with side-whiskers, being married to a lady all in white with a big bunch of flowers in her hand (that must have been difficult to cut out!); and the wreath of purple and blue and pink flowers, round a little landscape with a wonderful red sunset behind.

Oh, she had nearly forgotten how nice the scrap-work screen was inside!

There in the right-hand corner was the boy in the funny hat and red stockings leading by the hand the little girl in full skirts and tight boots. Bunchy thought that somehow the boy looked as if his name might be Hugh.

She crouched down on the floor close to him and touched his hand.

'Is your name Hugh?' she asked him.

'Yes,' he answered back directly; 'and this is my sister Rose. Won't you come in and walk with us?'

'Thank you,' said Bunchy; and, taking their two outstretched hands, she joined them in their bright little bit of country lane. 'Where is it you're going?'

'Today we are off to visit Miss Lucy, the young lady who skates,' said Hugh.

'And we are taking her these flowers,' said his sister, mincing along in her tight boots, 'so that perhaps she may lend us her skates.'

'That would be very nice!' said Bunchy, who had always wanted to skate.

They soon came to a stile into a cornfield, which was framed with poppies and cornflowers, and just the other side of that was the ice.

'Hold tight to me, Bunchy, or you may slip,' said the red-stockinged boy kindly; which Bunchy was very glad to do. And in another moment they were all sliding together over the ice, as fast as the wind!

On the other side of the pond the girl in the long red coat was skating gracefully around, her ringlets and the feathers in her hat swaying to and fro.

'How do you do? I'm glad you've come!' she said, as they got up to her. 'I'm quite tired of skating round all alone.' She seemed pleased to see Bunchy too. 'I've always wanted to know you,' she said; 'I knew your grandmother years ago.

They were all sliding together over the ice

Would you like to borrow my muff? You might feel cold here in that short dress.'

Bunchy was very glad of it. And then, because she was an honoured visitor, they let her borrow Miss Lucy's skates first.

They must have been wonderful skates, for Bunchy could use them straight away without any practice. She skimmed around the pond, feeling as if she were flying, holding Miss Lucy's soft white muff to her face. Indeed, she went so fast that she couldn't stop in time, and went right to the farther end of the pond, head first into a clump of great pink roses bordering the ice.

'Roses in winter-time?' thought Bunchy, sniffing their sweet scent. 'That's queer!' And then she remembered that the roses didn't belong to that picture at all – they were stuck on afterwards, when Grandmother was making the screen.

'You are not hurt, no?' said a slightly foreign voice; and the prettiest of the black-eyed Spanish young ladies looked over the flowers at her.

'Not at all, thank you!' said Bunchy, scrambling to her feet. 'I was just thinking of when Granny made this screen. I suppose you saw my granny and her sisters when they were young, didn't you? Do tell me, what were they like?'

'Not so pretty as I and my sisters, no, no!' said the Spanish lady conceitedly, smiling and tossing her head. 'Come, you must speak with them. Leave Miss Lucy's skates and muff there on the ice, where she can find them, and I will explain to her later.'

So Bunchy went with the lady where, near by the roses, the two other Spanish beauties were sitting fanning themselves, glancing this way and that out of their big dark eyes.

'Yes, we remember your grandmother quite well,' they told her. 'She was a nice girl, but ordinary, oh, quite ordinary! Not at all like *us*!' And they shook their satin skirts and their black lace headdresses in a satisfied way.

'I'm glad she wasn't like you,' thought Bunchy to herself; 'I'd much rather have a nice ordinary granny.' But aloud she only said, 'I think I must be going on now. Which way is the best?'

'That's a good way,' said the youngest young lady. So Bunchy went in the direction of her pointing fan, up a little winding path, by an ivy-grown church with a full moon just behind its steeple. Then she had to clamber over the silver horseshoe surrounding it all, out into a green field, where a big soldier in scarlet coat was standing, looking important, with his chest stuck out.

'Good day, Miss Bunchy,' said the soldier, twirling his moustache with finger and thumb. 'How is your respected grandmother today?'

'Quite well, thank you,' said Bunchy. 'Please, which is the best way to go from here?'

'It's rather a matter of opinion,' said the soldier; 'but that's not a bad way in front of you. Good day! Give my regards to your grandmother!' And with a smart salute he strutted off.

Bunchy went on to where some birds were standing by a great clump of primroses, watching a nest full of bright blue eggs.

There were two big thrushes, a little peacock and an ostrich.

'Whose nest is that?' asked Bunchy.

'Your grandmother's,' chirped the birds. 'She put it here, and we've been guarding it for nearly fifty years.'

'That's a long time!' said Bunchy.

Then she climbed up a pile of large books with an inkpot and a feather pen on the top; and when she had got safely down on the other side it was an easy jump from there to the floor of the cottage kitchen again.

'Goodbye, Hugh!' she said to the boy in the red stockings in the farther corner. 'Goodbye, Rose!' to the little girl in the tight boots; and she thought they waved back, but it was getting too dark to see.

'Granny,' she said, jumping up and going over to her grandmother's chair by the window, 'what were you like when you made that screen?'

'Very ordinary, my dear,' said Grandmother, smiling a little.

'But very nice!' said Bunchy, kissing her. 'Granny, did you wear red stockings?'

'No, white ones, and black boots,' said Grandmother.

'Like Rose, that girl in the corner there?'

'Something like her,' said Grandmother, 'only not so tight!'

BUNCHY
and the
HAPPY FAMILIES

ONCE upon a time the little girl named Bunchy was playing all by herself, as usual.

She had an old pack of cards, and was building houses on the floor, one storey, two storeys – and then the house would fall down flat, and she would have to start building it all over again.

Well, presently she gave up trying to make a high house, and made several little ones instead. They were easy. She made a row of them, and then she made another row, so that it looked just like a little street of houses.

'Only nobody lives in them,' said Bunchy; 'I wish they didn't have to be empty houses!'

Just at that moment Grandmother came into the room, and she had a little box in her hand.

'Look, Bunchy, my dear,' said Grandmother, 'what I have found in my old tin trunk in the attic – something I used to play with when I was a little girl! I had quite forgotten I still had them!'

Bunchy jumped up to look. And inside the box was a pack of funny old cards (you probably have some just like them now) called Happy Families.*

'Oh, Granny – what funny people!' Bunchy said, spreading the cards all out to look at them. 'Can I have them? Oh, thank you, Granny! They can come and live in my card houses – they'd like that, I expect!'

Bunchy did not know the game of Happy Families, and she had no one to play with if she did, for Grandmother was too busy, and anyhow, it's a game which needs more than two people to play.

But she settled down on the floor quite happily, for now her little row of card houses would have people to live in them: Mr Pots the Painter with Mrs Pots and Master and Miss Pots, in one; Mr Bones the Butcher and his wife and two children in another; and Mr Chip the Carpenter and his

* The title and characters of 'Happy Families' playing cards are used by kind permission of Messrs John Jaques and Son, Ltd, London, owners of the copyright.

family; there were so many families Bunchy had to do some more building to get them all housed. But at last there they were, all comfortable and busy as could be, each side of the little village street.

Bunchy was very interested indeed in all the little families. Miss Grits, the Grocer's Daughter, was the prettiest, she thought; but Mrs Block, the Barber's Wife, was the grandest. She looked as if she had a party dress on.

'*Are* you going to a party, Mrs Block?' asked Bunchy.

'Yes, we are giving a party at our house tonight,' said Mrs Block, opening her eyes very wide and fanning herself as she spoke. 'Perhaps you would like to have an invitation? Here is one for you.'

'Oh, thank you, ma'am,' said Bunchy; 'but I'm afraid I haven't a party dress to wear. I've only this one.'

'Well, I expect something could be done about that,' said Mrs Block. 'I tell you what – my friend, Mrs Pots, the Painter's Wife, always has good ideas about dresses and things. She'll tell you what to do. My daughter, Miss Block, shall take you – no, she can't go through the streets in that frock, it's too fine. My son, Master Block, shall go.'

So Master Block put down his comb and brush, and escorted Bunchy down the road to Mr Pots the Painter's house.

Mr Pots was outside painting the railings green, but Mrs Pots was inside the shop, looking rather gorgeous in a red-and-yellow striped dress with her hair done up artistically for the party. She had a bowl of paint and some brushes in her hands, which she put aside quickly when Bunchy came in, and Bunchy had an idea that she had been painting her ear-rings with it – and her cheeks too, for they were nearly as red. Little Miss Pots was painting *her* cheeks quite openly with a big brush, which Bunchy thought was rather silly; while Master Pots was licking away at another brush till he had made his tongue scarlet.

Master Block explained why he had brought Bunchy, and then went off home; and Mrs Pots very kindly considered what could be done with Bunchy's dress to make it more partyfied.

'I know,' said Mrs Pots at last. 'You could have your apron dyed red at Mr Dip the Dyer's, then it would look quite jolly. Yes, I think that's the very thing!'

Bunchy wasn't sure that she liked the idea very much, but she thanked Mrs Pots, and went in search of Mr Dip. She saw a boy with dripping blue hands grinning at her from a doorway, and she asked if Mr Dip lived there.

'Yes, he do,' said the boy. 'But you'd better be careful how you talk to my ma. I've been helping her to dye Miss Grits' dress for the party tonight, and now she's cross because she can't get the blue off her hands, and she says she won't be able to go to the party herself now. My hands don't matter, o' course – I wasn't invited, anyway. Come on in, if you want to see my pa.'

So Bunchy followed him into the dye-shop.

Mr Dip soon had her little white apron in a big tub of red dye, and Bunchy hardly knew it when he fetched it out again. He hung it up in his little backyard to dry; and Bunchy was quite glad when it was ready for her to take away, for Miss Dip, the Dyer's Daughter, had her nose in the air at the notion of Bunchy's going to the party at all in that dress.

Bunchy carried the parcel back to the Blocks' house. Mr Block, with his hair and whiskers most elaborately oiled and curled, met her at the door.

'Oh, Miss Bunchy,' he said, smiling and looking worried at the same time, 'would you very obligingly run to Mr Tape the Tailor's, and ask if he has finished mending my best suit? He promised to have it ready for tonight!'

So Bunchy ran off. She wasn't sure which was the Tailor's house, but she asked Master Bones, the Butcher's Son, whom she met delivering a joint; and then she opened the door and went in.

Mr Tape was sitting cross-legged on the floor sewing away as hard as he could go; and Mrs Tape was scolding Miss Tape because she hadn't tidied her hair yet, and wasn't to go out looking like *that*; and Master Tape was standing gloomily by with a big pair of scissors under his arm, hoping someone would find time to cut his shaggy locks before he went to the party.

'Please, is Mr Block the Barber's suit ready yet?' asked Bunchy at the door.

'Yes, just done, just done!' said Mr Tape hurriedly, breaking off his thread and rolling the garments into a parcel. 'There you are. Be quick back with them now.'

So Bunchy took them and ran all the way.

Mrs Block thanked her, and then asked if she would mind just going over to Mr Bun the Baker's and getting a couple more loaves, as she wasn't sure they had enough for the sandwiches for the party.

So Bunchy good-naturedly went.

Mrs and Miss Bun were both coming to the party later on, and served her in their best scarlet dresses – so Bunchy saw that her dyed apron was evidently the fashionable colour.

When she got back with the bread Mrs Block begged her to go across to Mr Grits the Grocer's for some more sugar.

Bunchy thought this was really getting rather much. However, she went; and pretty Miss Grits fetched a sugar-loaf, which Mr Grits obligingly weighed out for her. Master Grits, all clean and tidy, looked on, but Mrs Grits was still in her working-dress: she didn't think much of parties and such goings-on, and she was going to stay at home.

Well, this seemed to be the last errand, for when she got back little Miss Block took her up to her room and helped her to tidy and put on her red apron.

And then the party began to arrive.

And what a crowd there was! The Doses, the Dips, the Pots and the Grits, the Bones and the Chips: in fact, everybody who was not too young, or too disagreeable, or too grubby!

It was a very pleasant and interesting party indeed.

But what *do* you think? Right in the middle of it all, who should come marching in but Mr Soot the Sweep and all his family!

He said he had been sent for to sweep the chimneys; and sweep the chimneys he would, although Mr and Mrs Block protested loudly that they did not want him then, and had asked him to come *next* week.

He got to work with his long brushes (all his family helping), and the soot flew about till the

Who should come marching in but Mr Soot the Sweep!

guests were nearly choked. And so vigorous were they with their chimney-sweeping that they ended by pulling the whole card house down, *clatter, clatter, clatter,* over all their heads.

'Oh! Oh!' said Bunchy. 'All my nice card houses are knocked down! Oh, what a pity!'

'Never mind!' said Grandmother, putting the kettle on the range. 'It's just supper-time, and you would have had to take them down in another minute. Dear me, how this chimney smokes! I shall really have to send for the sweep next week.'

'I hope he won't knock our house down like Mr Soot did to all the card houses,' said Bunchy.

'Ah, I shan't send for your Mr Soot, then,' said Grandmother. 'Now tidy up the cards, dearie, and we'll lay the table for supper.'

BUNCHY and the SNOWSTORM BALL

ONCE upon a time the little girl named Bunchy was kneeling at the window in the kitchen of her grandmother's cottage, watching the rain come down. It poured and it poured, and all the leaves round the window were drip-drip-dripping, and the rain ran in little crooked trickles down the window-pane.

It was a very wet day indeed.

Grandmother had had to put on her big black waterproof cape, and her big black galoshes, and take her big black umbrella with her when she went outside to feed the chickens and to get a bucket of water from the pump. But it was much too wet for Bunchy to go and help her as usual. So all day Bunchy had had to stay indoors, doing her

little lessons and helping her grandmother in the
kitchen.

Now it wouldn't be very long before bedtime
came, and Bunchy was looking through the
window to see if there was any chance at all of
even a run just to the garden gate and back. But
there wasn't the least little bit.

'No, it's a stay-at-home day today, that's
certain,' said Grandmother, getting out her big
mending-basket.

'I wish there didn't have
to be stay-at-home days,'
said Bunchy. 'I've done
everything there is to do
indoors, Granny, and now
there isn't anything more –
not anything nice, I mean.'

'Oh, surely there's some-
thing nice we can find to
do before you go to bed,'
said Grandmother. 'I must
put on my thinking-cap!'

So Grandmother sewed thoughtfully for a
minute or two, and Bunchy watched her hopefully.

Then Grandmother put down her work and went
into the next room, which was the Best Parlour;

and Bunchy heard her open the little cupboard with the glass doors where the most precious ornaments were kept. When she came back she had in her hand a glass ball, which she put down on the windowsill beside Bunchy. 'There, my dearie!' said Grandmother. 'You may play with this for just a little while before bed, if you're very, very careful.'

'Oh, Granny,' said Bunchy, 'it's the snow-storm-ball! I'll be very, very careful, Granny, I promise! May I turn it upside-down first, just to start it properly?'

'Anything you like,' said Grandmother; 'but gently, you know.'

So Bunchy lifted the ball in her two hands, and turned it upside-down very gently indeed.

It was quite a heavy little glass ball with a small flat wooden stand fixed to the bottom; and Bunchy thought it was the most wonderful thing she had ever seen. For right inside the glass ball (and how it got there Bunchy couldn't imagine, for there was no opening anywhere to be seen) was a little snow-covered hill; and standing on the hill was a little red and white house, with a little green tree beside it, and a little road winding up to it; and on the road was a tiny little man holding up a tiny little umbrella.

But (most wonderful of all!) when you turned the ball upside-down and then stood it properly, snow came falling, softly, softly, on to the roof of the house, and on to the tree, and on to the ground, and on to the umbrella of the tiny little man.

But never a grain of it came outside the little glass ball.

Bunchy loved it more than any of her grandmother's ornaments, and was always excited whenever Grandmother set it up on the parlour mantelpiece for her to see. But now to have it all to her own self for a while seemed almost too good to believe.

Bunchy set the ball carefully down again on the windowsill, and leaned her chin there too, to watch. Down fell the snow, till the sky in the globe was filled with little whirling white flakes, settling slowly, slowly, all over the landscape and making it quite white.

'It's a good thing you've got an umbrella to put up,' said Bunchy to the little man inside.

'Indeed it is,' he answered her. 'I don't know what I should do without it, for it's nearly always snowing here. Such a place!'

'Yes,' said Bunchy; 'you must get dreadfully cold.'

'I do, sometimes,' said the little man. 'I think you're lucky to be able to stay indoors when it's raining. It snows so hard I can hardly get up the hill to my house. Look, it's almost burying me; only it never does quite. It always stops just in time.'

'Don't you ever go into your house?' asked Bunchy.

'Not while anyone is looking! But I go in at night, when it's all dark, and you can't see! I go up the hill, and I open the door, and I go in and shut it. And then I have a good warm-up, I can tell you!'

'Why don't you go in now?'

'Oh, but I couldn't while you're here! And suppose your grandmother were to come and find I was gone! She'd wonder wherever I was, and maybe she'd think I'd been broken. She wouldn't like that!'

'Look, the snow's stopping now,' said Bunchy.

'Yes, I have to stand in it up to my waist like this nearly all the time, and my umbrella gets so heavy with all the snow on it, you've no idea!'

'I'll shake it off,' said Bunchy. 'Wait a minute.' She shook the globe, and set the snow whirling round in the sky.

'My, what a storm!' said the little man, gripping his umbrella. 'I can hardly stand up against it. But I can see the road again, which is nice.'

'Why don't you go indoors for a bit?' asked Bunchy. 'Granny won't see you – she's busy. And she said I could play with you till bedtime. *I* don't mind if you go in. I think it would be a good thing.'

'Well, in that case perhaps I might,' said the little man, thoughtfully, '– if you're sure your grandmother won't see. It certainly would be nice to have a warm-up. Won't you come in with me? You'll have to run like anything, or you'll get covered with snow.'

'All right,' said Bunchy. And she ran up the little hill as fast as she could through the snow, with the little man staggering beside her with his snow-laden umbrella.

'Poof! That was hard work!' he panted, opening the door of his little house to let her in. He paused to close and shake his umbrella before he shut the door, and then he hung it up with his hat on a peg just inside, and turned to flick the snowflakes from Bunchy's dress and hair.

'It's nice to be indoors again, isn't it?' he said. 'Do sit down!'

So Bunchy sat down on a neat little chair by the flickering fire, and looked round the room.

It was just such a little room as you would imagine from seeing the outside of the house – low and snug, with white walls, and red-painted furniture, and a bright green carpet. The little log fire burned up brightly, the fire-irons were well polished, and the hearth was well swept. On the little red dresser were cups and plates, a shining kettle, and a cooking-pot; and let into the wall by the fireplace was a deep recess where a little bed was made up, with a plump pillow at one end and covered with a bright green coverlet.

The little man took off his boots and put on a pair of cosy red slippers which were warming for him on the hearth.

'Ah, this is very pleasant!' said the little man, leaning back in his chair. 'I don't often have a visitor in my little house. I'm very proud to see you here, I'm sure.'

Bunchy sat down and looked round the room

'It's a *very* comfortable house!' said Bunchy. 'I should love to live in a house like this. I don't wonder you want to get in out of the snow, sometimes!'

The little man looked delighted with her praise. 'I'm glad you like it!' he said. 'But don't let your grandmother think I am at all discontented with my lot, for she often comes to see me standing in the snow, and it is always a pleasure to me to see her. I should be very sorry not to be out there to greet her or any of her friends, any time they like to call.'

He got up, and, going to the little window, opened the shutter and peeped out. 'Everything's covered with snow again, but it's stopped falling now,' he said. 'Goodness me! I'm sure I hear your grandmother moving! You'd better go back quickly, or she will be wondering whatever has become of you – and of me too! Run, while I put on my boots and hat and get my umbrella! Goodbye!'

Bunchy jumped up and ran out of the little house as fast as she could go, down the snowy hillside, and got back to the cottage kitchen just as her grandmother rose from her chair, saying:

'Bedtime, Bunchy, my dear!'

'Oh, Granny, just let me say goodbye to the little man. I hadn't time to say "Thank you for having me"!' She looked at the glass ball. There was the little man outside his house with his umbrella up, braving the cold as usual.

'I'm glad I don't have to stay outside all the time, like him,' she said, as her grandmother took up the ball to put it back in her cabinet. 'It's much nicer to be indoors when it's raining or snowing, isn't it, Granny? But I hope it will be fine tomorrow, so that I can go out! Do you think it will be?'

'Yes,' said Grandmother. 'The sunset was quite red. I think it will be fine tomorrow.'

BUNCHY and the CLOTHES PEGS

ONCE upon a time the little girl called Bunchy was playing alone in the garden, for her grandmother was busy in the cottage kitchen, ironing the clothes. Bunchy was just wandering round, smelling the different flowers and looking to see what new ones were opening, rather wondering to herself what she could do next, when Grandmother came to the back door.

'Bunchy!' called Grandmother. 'Will you gather up the clothes pegs for me? I dropped them all over the grass when I brought in the washing in that shower yesterday. Just put them all tidily into this basket, will you, my dear?'

'Yes, Granny!' said Bunchy.

And she took the basket and ran along the little path to the grassy patch at the side of the cottage, where the clothes-lines stretched from tree to tree, and where, every week, the frocks and the socks and the aprons and all the other things that Grandmother washed hung flapping themselves dry in the nice, clean wind.

There were only one or two cloths dangling there now, twitching at their pegs as if they wanted to get away; but on the ground below there were quite a number of other pegs lying about. One was propped against a tuft of grass as if it were trying to stand up on its two little wooden legs. As she picked it up, Bunchy thought that it looked like a funny little man, with its little round wooden knob of a head. She took up another.

'They all look like little men-pegs,' she said to herself. 'If some of them had skirts then there would be little lady-pegs too. I wonder . . . '

She looked around.

By the wall there grew a great clump of California poppies, and some of the flowers were beginning to drop. Bunchy picked up two or three of the big shiny red petals from the grass and arranged them round the clothes peg in her hand, tying them round its waist with a piece of ribbon-grass.

The peg looked just like a little lady in a scarlet satin skirt, and Bunchy, delighted, stuck it in the ground so that it stood up by itself while she stepped back to admire it.

And then – what *do* you think? – why, the little clothes-peg lady began to twirl slowly round in a stiff little dance, while Bunchy watched, wide-eyed! It spread its scarlet petal skirts, using the two ends of the grass-blade sash as if they were arms, and kicked with its little wooden legs in the liveliest way; and at that moment the first clothes peg jumped out of the basket and came stalking solemnly forward, one stiff leg at a time.

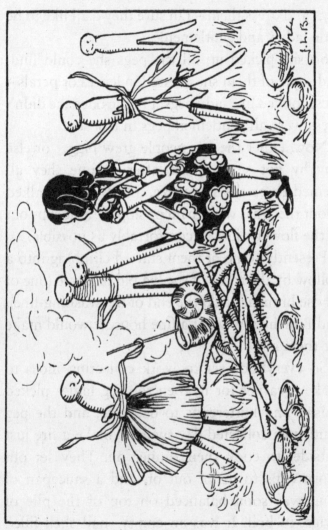

The peg people crowded round

'Oh!' said Bunchy; then, 'I must find some more pegs and dress them – I'm sure they'd all like to be little ladies and gentlemen!'

So she picked up all the pegs she could find, and some of them she dressed in leaves or petals – these looked like lady pegs; but the ones she didn't dress were all gentlemen pegs in trousers.

Now, either the peg people grew bigger or else Bunchy got smaller, for after a time they all seemed to be the same size, and Bunchy walked about the grass with them or sipped raindrops out of the flowers, just as comfortably as possible.

Presently some of them started climbing into a hollow by the roots of the big old oak tree (one of whose branches held the end of the washing-line), and Bunchy saw what a fine house it would make for them all.

So everybody set to work collecting moss to make a carpet for it; then the peg ladies picked daisies and buttercups to decorate, and the peg gentlemen collected dry twigs to make a fire just outside, to cook their dinner on. They set out acorn cups to drink out of, and a saucepan of soup was soon balanced on top of the pile of twigs, to boil. It was an empty snail shell filled with something that looked rather like mud and water, but all the peg people seemed to think it was very delicious, by the way they crowded round.

The cloths still hanging on the line were flapping about just above them, and Bunchy began to think that they really were flapping quite extraordinarily wildly; and then suddenly the pegs holding one of them fell off the line, and ran towards the little party round the fire, as if they just couldn't or wouldn't hold on any longer with such good things going on so near them.

'Oh, you naughty pegs!' cried Bunchy, jumping up to pick up the cloth. 'You *must* hold the cloths on the line, or they'll get so dirty! Come here at once!'

But the little pegs wouldn't come, no matter how she called; they were much too busy pouring soup from the snail-shell pot into their acorn-cup bowls to attend to her!

'Oh, dear!' said Bunchy, looking at the cloth in her hand. 'I'm sure Granny wouldn't like this to be left on the grass, but I can't reach the line to fix it up, even if those naughty pegs hadn't run off like that!'

Just then the first little lady peg in the poppy-petal skirt came tripping across the grass and took hold of one corner of the cloth, beckoning to Bunchy meanwhile with one of her grass-blade arms.

'What are you going to do?' asked Bunchy, following.

The little peg pulled her along to the oak tree and climbed nimbly up, still holding one end of the cloth; and Bunchy climbed up after, holding on to the other. When the peg reached the branch to which the clothes-line was tied, it ran out a little way along it like a tiny tightrope dancer, pulling Bunchy along after her; then, settling the cloth on the line, she sat down on it, pegged it firmly on, and beckoned to Bunchy to do the same with her end.

'Well!' said Bunchy to herself, though feeling

rather dismayed. 'I've got two legs like a peg, so I suppose I can do it.'

And she sat awkwardly down, trying to fix the cloth on to the line and to balance herself at the same time.

It wasn't at all comfortable, but then, of course, she was very new at it: the wind flapped the cloth and jerked the clothes-line so alarmingly at times that it was all she could do to hold on.

And then, just as she was beginning to get used to her queer position, what *do* you think that naughty little peg on the other side of the cloth did?

It leaned sideways till it got its leg nearly over the line, and then with the next puff of wind it dropped to the ground and ran to join its companions, leaving Bunchy to keep the cloth pegged to the line all by herself!

'Peggy! Come back!' called Bunchy, jigging wildly up and down with the flapping of the cloth beneath her, but still holding tightly on: for the line was some way from the ground, and her head was not just a wooden knob like most pegs – besides, the cloth would get so dirty if it fell down a second time.

'Oh, dear – this *is* a bother!' thought Bunchy, swaying this way and that in the wind. 'Those naughty little pegs!'

Just then a drop of rain splashed on to her head. 'Dear, dear, dear!' thought Bunchy. 'Whatever shall I do? It's going to rain, and I shall get soaked, and so will the cloth!'

At that moment she heard her grandmother's voice calling, 'Bunchy! Where are you? Come along in out of the rain!' And down she came to earth with a bump!

'Yes, Granny!' she cried. 'Oh, Granny, there's a cloth on the ground; what shall I do with it?'

'Bring it in quickly!' said Grandmother.

So Bunchy picked up the cloth, and hastily threw the pegs into the basket and ran indoors with them.

'Look, Granny, at the little peg lady!' she said, holding one up. 'I shouldn't like to be a peg person. It must be a bother to have to hold clothes on to a line all day long, mustn't it?'

'Not if you were a peg,' said Grandmother. 'It's their work, you know, and it's nice to be useful. Now help me to lay the table for dinner!'

'Yes, Granny!' said Bunchy. 'That's more my sort of work than pegging clothes, isn't it, Granny?'

BUNCHY and the PEDDLER'S DOLL

ONCE upon a time the little girl named Bunchy was playing all by herself in the garden, with the old wooden tub that used to be her grandmother's wash-tub before it got too old.

It was green and mossy, for it had been lying under the hawthorn hedge all the winter, and it was half full of rain water and drowned leaves. Bunchy was amusing herself by scooping them out, and letting the water shine clear and brown in the bottom. And then she floated little daisy-heads on it like water-lilies.

It was a pretty sort of lake, Bunchy thought, dabbling her hand in it and watching the drops sparkle in the sun.

Just then someone came trudge-trudging along the lane the other side of the low brick wall, and Bunchy looked up from her tub. And who do you think it was? Why, the old peddler-man, with his pack on his back, and his tray in front, and his stick in his hand.

And he came along, *trudge-trudge*, up to the little gate of the cottage and pushed it open; and he went *trudge-trudge*, two steps along the little brick path up to the front door, which was standing ajar. And he called out, as if it were poetry:

'Anything from the peddler today, ma'am?
Any pins, needles, buttons, or hooks?
Any tape, string, cotton, or darning wool?
Here's everything to your needs!'

Bunchy ran up to see what her grandmother would buy.

And Grandmother, when she had found her purse, bought a card of linen buttons and two reels of cotton, black and white.

Then the old peddler-man said, 'Now, I've got sommat here as might interest you, ma'am,' and he twisted his pack round and felt down deep into

it. And he brought out a little, blue, wooden –
what do you think? – a little, blue, wooden
sailor doll, with jointed arms.

'O-oh, Granny!' said Bunchy, staring at it very
hard.

The old peddler-man turned it round in his
fingers, and he twisted its arms up and down, and
it really looked a very lively little sailor-man.

'How much?' asked Grandmother at last, after
looking at Bunchy's face.

'One penny, ma'am, and you might pay
tuppence for it anywhere and not be cheated,'
said the old peddler-man, still turning the sailor
doll slowly round before Bunchy's eyes.

So Grandmother, after thinking a moment, took out another penny from her purse and gave it to the old peddler-man; and then she took the sailor doll and gave it to Bunchy.

'Oh, Granny! Oh, thank you!' said Bunchy; and she hardly noticed when the old peddler-man wished them 'Good morning,' and trudge-trudged again on his way up the lane.

'Isn't he a sweet little sailor-man!' said Bunchy. 'Granny, sailor-men always live on the sea, don't they? I'd better put him in that old tub in the garden, hadn't I? He'd like that, wouldn't he, Granny?'

'Just the thing,' agreed her grandmother. 'He should have a boat to sail in, though. I'll make you a paper one.'

So kind Grandmother went into the cottage; and she got a piece of paper, and while Bunchy watched, she folded it and folded it till it looked like a cocked hat; then she folded it again till it looked like a smaller cocked hat. Then she gave it a little pull and a little poke, and there it was – a paper boat, all ready for a little blue wooden sailor-man to sail in.

'Oh, thank you, Granny!' said Bunchy, and she ran out to the old tub under the hawthorn hedge.

She put the little sailor in the boat, and set it carefully down on the water, and it *floated* – and the little sailor-man looked so happy with his arm up, waving to her!

'Well!' said Bunchy, throwing in bits of leaves to look like fishes, and a knobbly piece of tree-root for a whale. 'It must be nice to be back on the sea again, after being in that peddler-man's pack all that time.'

'Oh, it is!' said the sailor. 'It was dreadful in there, you can't think. So dark. And stuffy! And I'm so used to the open air, you know.'

'Yes, indeed,' said Bunchy, dipping in her fingers to make little waves to rock the boat a bit, 'sailors always are.'

'Would you care to come for a sail with me?' asked the little sailor, jigging up and down quite easily on the waves. 'It's rather rough, but you needn't be afraid. I'm so used to all sorts of weather, I'll look after you.'

'Oh, thank you,' said Bunchy, 'I should love to come for a sail with you.' So the sailor-man steered his boat to the side, and Bunchy jumped into it.

It wasn't a very comfortable boat to sit in, but it did well enough.

It wasn't a very comfortable boat

'Look, what a lot of fishes!' said Bunchy, peering over the edge.

'Yes,' said the little sailor, 'we might catch some for our dinner. Here is a fishing-rod for you.' He handed her a bit of stick, and together they sat and fished and fished till they got a number of fishes, fine big ones, in the boat.

Presently, 'Oh!' cried Bunchy. 'I've got a great big fish! Oh! It's an enormous great one – I can't pull it up. Come and help me!'

So the little sailor came over to her side, and they pulled and they pulled, but they couldn't get it up. Then they looked down over the edge of the boat, and Bunchy exclaimed:

'I do believe it's a whale. Oh dear, oh dear, what shall we do?'

'Hold on!' cried the sailor bravely. 'He may upset the boat, and we are in the middle of the sea, a long way from land.'

So Bunchy and the sailor held on to the fishing-rod, while the whale plunged up and down, rocking the little boat from side to side, so that she thought every minute they would be thrown out. The waves rose till they splashed into the boat.

'Don't be afraid,' cried the sailor. 'I have had worse shipwrecks than this.'

'Oh, we've let go of the rod!' cried Bunchy. 'Now the whale has escaped. I hope he won't come back again.'

'He might come at any time,' said the sailor. 'He might try to eat us up. He's very cross at nearly being caught.'

'Oh, I do hope he won't,' said Bunchy, shivering. 'I got very wet with those big waves, did you?'

'Yes, and I think the boat's leaking,' said the sailor, feeling about. 'Yes, it's all soft and rotten here, and the water's coming in.'

'It's *pouring* in,' cried Bunchy. 'Oh, oh, we're sinking!'

'We must swim to the shore,' shouted the sailor. 'It's a lot of miles, but I expect we can do it.'

At that moment the boat filled rapidly and sank beneath them, and they were left in the water among the floating daisy-heads. 'Swim!' cried the sailor boldly. 'I'm here!'

So Bunchy swam and swam, but it seemed as if they would never reach the shore. Presently she saw a brown rock sticking out of the water, and she swam to it and was going to climb on it to rest awhile. But suddenly it moved, and she saw it was not a rock at all.

'Oh, sailor, it's the whale! Help!' she shouted, splashing hard.

But the whale said, 'It's all right – don't be frightened. Get on my back and I will take you home.'

So Bunchy said, 'Oh, thank you very much!' and scrambled up. And in a moment the kind whale had swum with her to the edge of the old wooden tub, and she managed to pull herself over the rim down on to the grass again.

'Come along, dinner's just ready,' called Grandmother from the back door. 'Now what have you been doing?'

'I was shipwrecked, Granny – look at the poor boat,' said Bunchy, fetching it up, dripping and shapeless, from the bottom of the tub. 'And I swam, and I swam. And a whale took me on his back. That's the whale, Granny.' She held up the bit of tree-root.

'And where is your sailor?' asked Grandmother.

'He's still swimming home. Look, there he is; doesn't he swim nicely? He's got very wet.'

'It seems to me *you've* got very wet,' said Grandmother, looking her over, 'all down the front of your pinafore!'

'Oh, Granny, I'm sorry. It's hard to remember about keeping dry when you're being shipwrecked.'

Grandmother laughed, and gave her a little tap. 'Run along, my dearie, or dinner will be getting cold,' she said.

Extra!

Extra!

READ ALL ABOUT IT!

JOYCE LANKESTER BRISLEY

Bunchy

A PUFFIN BOOK

1896   Born 6 February in Bexhill-on-Sea, Sussex

1909   Joyce has her first fairy story published in a
        children's paper when she is only thirteen
        years old

1912   Joyce and her sister Nina enrol at the Lambeth
        School of Art in London and supplement the
        family income by writing stories and illustrating
        Christmas cards, postcards and children's annuals

1916   Some of Joyce's pictures are displayed in the
        Royal Academy of Arts in London

1925   Her first story about Milly-Molly-Mandy is
        printed in the USA by the Christian Science
        Monitor magazine

1928–1967	*The first collection of Milly-Molly-Mandy stories is published in the UK in 1928 by George G. Harrap & Company Ltd, and the series goes on to become her most famous creation*
1938	*Joyce illustrates* The Adventures of the Little Wooden Horse *by Ursula Moray Williams*
1937	Bunchy *is published*
1951	*Another Bunchy collection of adventures is published*
1978	*Dies at the age of eighty-two*

INTERESTING FACTS

Joyce both wrote and illustrated her books. The Milly-Molly-Mandy series deservedly became her most well-loved and famous creation.

She had two sisters, named Nina and Ethel, who were also illustrators.

The Happy Families card game with which Bunchy plays has been around since 1851.

GUESS WHO?

A ... smiling and twinkling at her in the friendliest way possible!

B ... put on her cloak and her bonnet, her galoshes and her mittens, took her big basket and her big umbrella, and set forth.

C He had to speak in rather an odd sort of voice because his mouth had been drawn crooked.

D ... she threw button jewels, which the toys gathered up and took home, and were rich for life!

E 'It's hard to remember about keeping dry when you're being shipwrecked.'

QUIZ

1 **What does Buttercup nearly do with Grandmother's 'diamonds'?**

a) *Hide them*

b) *Steal them*

c) *Throw them out of the window*

d) *Put them in the bin*

2 **What colour does Mr Dip the Dyer dye Bunchy's apron?**

a) *Blue*

b) *Red*

c) *Green*

d) *White*

3 What does Bunchy make her first clothes-peg doll's skirt out of?

a) *Poppy petals*

b) *A cupcake case*

c) *Leaves*

d) *Grass*

4 What does Grandmother buy for Bunchy from the old peddler-man?

a) *A book*

b) *A dress*

c) *A china doll*

d) *A wooden sailor doll*

5 Who helps Bunchy swim home when she is shipwrecked?

a) *A whale*

b) *A dolphin*

c) *A turtle*

d) *A fisherman*

WORDS GLORIOUS WORDS!

Lots of words have several different meanings – here are a few you'll find in this Puffin book. Use a **dictionary** or look them up online to find other definitions.

muff *a fur tube for keeping your hands warm*

conceited *having a high opinion of oneself*

errand *a short journey or small favour or task, particularly one done for somebody else*

vigorous *full of energy*

coverlet *a bedcover*

peddler *a person who sells small goods door to door; a more usual spelling of this word in British English is 'pedlar'*

MAKE
AND
DO

Make your own peg doll!

YOU WILL NEED:

* Wooden dolly pegs
* Clear nail polish
* A marker pen
* Paper fairy-cake cases
* Pipe cleaners
* Sticky tape

1 Paint the head of the dolly peg with clear nail polish. Leave to dry and then draw on a face with the marker pen.

2 Fold a fairy-cake case in half and cut a small slit at the top of the fold. Open it up and carefully slide it on to the doll to make a skirt. Secure at the back with some sticky tape.

3 Cut one pipe cleaner to about 15 cm long to make the arms.

4 Wrap the pipe cleaner round the peg just below the doll's head so that it hangs down equally on both sides. Turn up the ends of the pipe cleaner to make hands.

5 Your doll is now ready to play! Why not make a whole family?

IN THIS YEAR

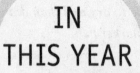

1937
Fact Pack

What else was happening in the world when this book was first published?

George **VI** *becomes king of England.*

Walt Disney's first movie, **Snow White and the Seven Dwarfs,** *is released in cinemas.*

The ***first frozen food*** *appears British shops.*

The first **Dr Seuss** *book,* And to Think That I Saw It on Mulberry Street, *is published.*

PUFFIN WRITING TIP

Get lost in your imagination and make friends with the people you find there!

If you have enjoyed *Bunchy*, you may like to read *Stuart Little* by E. B. White, all about a little mouse with a very adventurous spirit.

6. A Fair Breeze

ONE morning when the wind was from the west, Stuart put on his sailor suit and his sailor hat, took his spyglass down from the shelf, and set out for a walk, full of the joy of life and the fear of dogs. With a rolling gait he sauntered along toward Fifth Avenue, keeping a sharp lookout.

Whenever he spied a dog through his glass, Stuart would hurry to the nearest doorman, climb his trouserleg, and hide in the tails of his uniform. And once, when no doorman

was handy, he had to crawl into a yesterday's paper and roll himself up in the second section till danger was past.

At the corner of Fifth Avenue there were several people waiting for the uptown bus, and Stuart joined them. Nobody noticed him, because he wasn't tall enough to be noticed.

'I'm not tall enough to be noticed,' thought Stuart, 'yet I'm tall enough to want to go to Seventy-second Street.'

When the bus came into view, all the men waved their canes and briefcases at the driver, and Stuart waved his spyglass. Then, knowing that the step of the bus would be too high for him, Stuart seized hold of the cuff of a gentleman's pants and was swung aboard without any trouble or inconvenience whatever.

Stuart never paid any fare on buses, because he wasn't big enough to carry an ordinary dime. The only time he had ever attempted to carry a dime, he had rolled the coin along like

a hoop while he raced along beside it; but it had got away from him on a hill and had been snatched up by an old woman with no teeth. After that experience Stuart contented himself with the tiny coins which his father made for him out of tin foil. They were handsome little things, although rather hard to see without putting on your spectacles.

When the conductor came around to collect the fares, Stuart fished in his purse and pulled out a coin no bigger than the eye of a grasshopper.

'What's that you're offering me?' asked the conductor.

'It's one of my dimes,' said Stuart.

'Is it, now?' said the conductor. 'Well, I'd have a fine time explaining that to the bus company. Why, you're no bigger than a dime yourself.'

'Yes I am,' replied Stuart angrily. 'I'm more than twice as big as a dime. A dime only comes up to here on me.' And Stuart pointed to his hip. 'Furthermore,' he added, 'I didn't come on this bus to be insulted.'

'I beg pardon,' said the conductor. 'You'll have to forgive me, for I had no idea that in all the world there was such a small sailor.'

'Live and learn,' muttered Stuart, tartly, putting his change purse back in his pocket.

When the bus stopped at Seventy-second Street, Stuart jumped out and hurried across to the sailboat pond in Central Park. Over the pond the west wind blew, and into the teeth of the west wind sailed the sloops and

schooners, their rails well down, their wet decks gleaming. The owners, boys and grown men, raced around the cement shores hoping to arrive at the other side in time to keep the boats from bumping. Some of the toy boats were not as small as you might think, for when you got close to them you found that their mainmast was taller than a man's head, and they were beautifully made, with everything shipshape and ready for sea. To Stuart they seemed enormous, and he hoped he would be able to get aboard one of them and sail away to the far corners of the pond. (He was an adventurous little fellow and loved the feel of the breeze in his face and the cry of the gulls overhead and the heave of the great swell under him.)

As he sat cross-legged on the wall that surrounds the pond, gazing out at the ships through his spyglass, Stuart noticed one boat that seemed to him finer and prouder than any other. Her name was *Wasp*. She was a big, black schooner flying the American flag. She had a clipper bow, and on her foredeck was mounted a three-inch cannon. She's the ship for me, thought Stuart. And the next time she

sailed in, he ran over to where she was being turned around.

'Excuse me, sir,' said Stuart to the man who was turning her, 'but are you the owner of the schooner *Wasp*?'

'I am,' replied the man, surprised to be addressed by a mouse in a sailor suit.

'I'm looking for a berth in a good ship,' continued Stuart, 'and I thought perhaps you might sign me on. I'm strong and I'm quick.'

'Are you sober?' asked the owner of the *Wasp*.

'I do my work,' said Stuart, crisply.

The man looked sharply at him. He couldn't help admiring the trim appearance and bold manner of this diminutive seafaring character.

'Well,' he said at length, pointing the prow of the *Wasp* out toward the centre of the pond, 'I'll tell you what I'll do with you. You see that big racing sloop out there?'

'I do,' said Stuart.

'That's the *Lillian B. Womrath*,' said the man, 'and I hate her with all my heart.'

'Then so do I,' cried Stuart, loyally.

'I hate her because she is always bumping into my boat,' continued the man, 'and because her owner is a lazy boy who doesn't understand sailing and who hardly knows a squall from a squid.'

'Or a jib from a jibe,' cried Stuart.

'Or a luff from a leech,' bellowed the man.

'Or a deck from a dock,' screamed Stuart.

'Or a mast from a mist,' yelled the man. 'But hold on, now, no more of this! I'll tell you what we'll do. The *Lillian B. Womrath* has always been able to beat the *Wasp* sailing, but I believe that if my schooner were properly handled it would be a different story. Nobody knows how I suffer, standing here on shore, helpless, watching the *Wasp* blunder along, when all she needs is a steady hand on her helm. So, my young friend, I'll let you sail the *Wasp* across the pond and back, and if you can beat that detestable sloop I'll give you a regular job.'

'Aye, aye, sir!' said Stuart, swinging himself aboard the schooner and taking his place at the wheel. 'Ready about!'

'One moment,' said the man. 'Do you mind telling me *how* you propose to beat the other boat?'

Stuart Little is available in **A Puffin Book**.